Little Wave and Old Swell

Little Wave and Old Swell

A Fable of Life and Its Passing

Jim Ballard

Foreword by Ken Blanchard

ATRIA BOOKS
New York London Toronto Sydney

BEYOND WORDS
PUBLISHING

BEYOND WORDS PUBLISHING

ATRIA BOOKS
A Division of Simon & Schuster, Inc.
1230 Avenue of the Americas
New York, NY 10020

20827 N.W. Cornell Road, Suite 500
Hillsboro, Oregon 97124-9808
503-531-8700 tel
503-531-8773 fax
www.beyondword.com

Managing editors: Henry Covi, Lindsay S. Brown
Proofreaders: Jessica Bryan and Marvin Moore
Illustrator: Catherine M. Elliott
Cover, interior design, and composition: Carol Sibley

First Atria Books/Beyond Words hardcover edition June 2007

For more information about special discounts for bulk purchases,
please contact Simon & Schuster Special Sales at
1-800-456-6798 or business@simonandschuster.com.

Manufactured in Mexico

10 9 8 7 6 5 4 3 2 1

Library of Congress Cataloging-in-Publication Data

Ballard, Jim

  Little Wave and Old Swell : a fable of life and its passing / Jim Ballard ; inspired by Paramahansa Yogananda ; foreword by Ken Blanchard.—1st ed.
       p.   cm.
  1. Life—Religious aspects—Self-Realization Fellowship. 2. Death—Religious aspects—Self-Realization Fellowship. I. Yogananda, Paramahansa, 1893–1952. II. Title.
  BP605.S4B35 2006
  158—dc22

                                    2006000151

ISBN-13: 978-1-58270-141-7 (hardcover)
ISBN-10:   1-58270-141-5 (hardcover)

The corporate mission of Beyond Words Publishing, Inc.: *Inspire to Integrity*

Lovingly dedicated to the matchless one
whose precepts have given birth to
this little story

Contents

Foreword
viii

one
The Journey
1

two
The Game
17

three
The Lesson
29

four
The Storm
41

five
A New Name
53

six
Destiny
67

Foreword

Over the more than thirty years of our friendship, Jim Ballard and I have been inspired and enriched by sharing insights from our separate spiritual journeys. While I have been drawn to the feet of the Master of Galilee, Jim has followed the meditation path taught by Paramahansa Yogananda, the great Indian teacher. In more than one of the books we have coauthored, Jim has tapped the writings of his guru. Now, in a simple folktale-type allegory, he uses Yogananda's metaphor of human life as a wave that rises and falls on the Ocean of God as a means of addressing the most basic questions all of us ask.

Some people might ask why a follower of Jesus is writing the foreword for a book inspired by an Indian guru. The fact is, Yogananda loved Jesus, and Jesus would have loved Yogananda. Every year, the Self-Realization Fellowship headquarters in Los Angeles—as well as all of its temples and meditation groups throughout the world—hold a full-day

Christmas event. It is a time of reverent reflection, with periodic interruptions to listen to taped messages of Yogananda's love for Jesus and his teachings. The way I see it, love is love.

There's an old saying, "We don't grow up; we just get taller." *Little Wave and Old Swell* is a book for the innocent seeker in each of us, young or old. It's a book to read alone with contemplation. It's a tale to tell to children. And it can be a gift of hope to someone in bereavement. The experiences of Little Wave remind us of how easy it is in this rush-around world to be caught up in the noisy excitement and competitive actions that lead only to exhaustion. How difficult it can be to stop and calm ourselves.

Reading *Little Wave*, I'm reminded of a favorite saying of mine: "Life is a very special occasion." Enjoy this story. Read it many times. Let it speak to your heart.

Ken Blanchard

one

The Journey

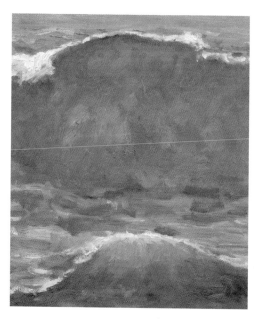

"What is it, Old Swell?" Little Wave
asked his teacher.

Little Wave was gazing out at the place where the sky and sea meet.

He had seen other things rising out there—
clouds and ships and whales. But never had
he seen anything like the long, dark line
that lay across the horizon.

Old Swell knew that Little Wave had never seen land and that he would not understand. So he answered like the sage he was. "That," said Old Swell, "is *Destiny*."

"What is Destiny?" Little Wave asked. But his teacher was silent.

Ever since Little Wave could remember,
Old Swell had been there to guide him
on the voyage they were making together.
Old Swell called it the *Journey*.

Throughout the Journey, Old Swell
had given Little Wave wise counsel and
loving protection. The sage taught him
many secrets. Every day there were new
lessons to learn.

But it was Old Swell's company that blessed Little Wave the most. Just being around his teacher calmed and comforted him.

When he was in Old Swell's presence, his cares melted away, and his world felt secure.

Little Wave tried to be good and do what Old Swell said, but he was often bored. He wanted something to do. He wanted to move faster. He wanted things to happen!

He found it hard to concentrate, especially when the Ruffles came to play.

Old Swell often cautioned
Little Wave against playing
with the Ruffles.

"They will only bring you
trouble," he said.

But the Ruffles, those patterns of darker water agitated by the breeze, fascinated Little Wave.

He felt excited whenever he saw them shimmer across the surface of the sea.

Little Wave waited quietly for the lesson he thought would come. Wondering at his teacher's long silence, he looked at Old Swell. He noticed that Old Swell's surface had become smooth and glassy.

He knew then that his teacher was doing what he called *Deep Listening*. He was concentrating on what he called the *Sound*.

As he watched Old Swell, Little Wave wondered what the Sound was like.

Whenever he had tried to do Deep Listening himself, he heard nothing but the wail of the wind, the cry of a sea bird, or the wash of nearby waves.

Just then a gust of wind brought
a band of Ruffles across his path.

Before Little Wave could alter
his course, the impish Ruffles had
covered him and were agitating
his surface.

"Stop it," gurgled Little Wave.
"That tickles!"

He arched his back and shook
himself, but the Ruffles would not
leave him alone.

"Come and play with us," they
hissed invitingly.

"I can't," Little Wave murmured.
"I have to stay with my teacher."

"Suit yourself," the Ruffles said, their voices seeming to pull at Little Wave. "But we can show you things!"

"What kinds of things?" Little Wave asked, suddenly interested.

"Things of wonder and delight," the naughty little Ruffles crooned. "Come on!"

"Where are these things?" Little Wave asked.

"Right over there in that sun-puddle."

Little Wave was excited; he wanted to see the wonderful things. He began moving away from Old Swell. *I'll just go and look for a minute*, he told himself.

two

The Game

The Ruffles led Little Wave to a broad patch of sea that was reflecting a beam of sunlight streaming down through an opening in the clouds.

"Look at those sun-sparkles," his playmates exclaimed. "Have you ever seen such a sight? Aren't they beautiful?"

Little Wave
was dazzled
by the sight
of millions of
glints of light
dancing about
on the path
made by the
sun.

Just then another wave, his friend
Foamy, came along. "Hi, Little Wave,"
he called. "Let's play the Glitter Game!"

"How do you play?" Little Wave asked.

"You gather all the sun-sparkles you can,"
Foamy explained, "and I do the same.
The one with the most sparkles wins."

Little Wave was entranced by the sight of all the sun-sparkles and the idea of getting more of them. He moved out into the glistening patch of light.

Soon he had surrounded a great horde of sparkles. Herding them into the hollow under his crest, he surged away after more.

"This is fun!" he shouted. As he dashed about, he became more excited and felt he could never have enough of those gorgeous glints.

The more sparkles he gathered, the more he wanted.

"Get more! Get more!" Foamy cried.

Soon Little Wave took up the chant:
"Get more! Get more! Get more!"
His whole mind became filled with
the shimmer of gold.

After the two had played for a long
time, Foamy called out jeeringly,
"I've got lots more sparkles than you!"

Little Wave felt a surge of jealousy.
"Oh yeah?" he shouted. He tore about
more frantically than before, gathering
more great throngs of sparkles.

It was no longer a game. Little Wave felt
he *must* outdo Foamy! He had all the
sparkles he could hold, but the faster he
gathered them, the faster they slipped
away. But still he tried for more.

Then without warning, the sun
went behind a cloud. In a moment,
all the sparkles were gone.
Little Wave stopped and looked around,
but Foamy was nowhere to be seen.
Little Wave was alone.

As he made his way back to Old Swell,
he felt empty and exhausted.

On the way home, Little Wave looked again
at the dark line Old Swell called Destiny.
He was sure that it was coming closer.

Soon he was back where he belonged, but it took a long time for his waters to stop roiling and swirling.

three

The Lesson

"Master," Little Wave spoke humbly,
"tell me again what Deep Listening means."

"First," said the sage, "you must be still."

"How can a wave be still?"

"Look not at appearances. The outside is only a show. Let your mind go beneath the surface."

Little Wave was doubtful. When he had tried this before, he'd found himself distracted or bored and unable to concentrate.

He resolved to try again. Instead of looking at the surface of the sea, as he always did, or at the dark shape approaching on the horizon line, he looked within. Instead of listening to the familiar sound of the waves, he directed his attention inside, down into the *Great Deep*.

And there he saw something
he had never noticed before.

Below his surface, a silent parade was passing. Through his waters floated bubbles, jellyfish, plankton, tiny plants, and other objects large and small.

Little Wave became fascinated as he watched the stream of things moving below him. He had been observing them for a long time when something strange happened.

He saw that the objects only *seemed* to be floating by. In reality, they were not moving at all. The water in which they floated was not moving, either!

In a flash, the way Little Wave looked at his world was changed.

If my waters stay where they are, then what is it that moves? What is a wave, anyway?

As he pondered this mystery, Little Wave felt
a strange, deep contentment. Perhaps this was
what Old Swell meant by being still.

By questioning his true nature as a wave he was
being drawn toward something wonderful.

What am I, really? he thought.

Old Swell was watching, and he read
Little Wave's mind.

"You are a moving wrinkle on the seamless fabric of the Great Deep," he said. "You thought that you were separate, but *no*. You can never be apart from your Source.

"Know that you and I and all of our brother and sister waves are One with the Great Deep.

"We have always been One.
We shall always be One."

Night came, clear and warm. The stars twinkled in the heavens, and the moon laid a glistening silver path on the sea.

Somewhere off in the distance the thing called Destiny was coming closer, but Little Wave was at peace. He was listening to Old Swell sing his favorite song:

From Joy I came.
In Joy I live,
And in Thy sacred Joy
I will melt again.

four

The Storm

The next morning, as he went to check the approach of Destiny, Little Wave saw that the horizon was completely covered in a thick mist.

The sky off in the west turned dark with angry-looking clouds. Lightning flashed, thunder rumbled, and a slanting curtain of rain descended.

As Little Wave watched, he felt something
like goose bumps ripple across his back.
He knew that feeling; the Ruffles were back!

"Go away," he told them.

"See that storm?" they urged. "Let's go play
in it!"

"I won't," Little Wave protested.

"You don't know how exciting it is!" hissed the Ruffles.

"But it looks scary," Little Wave objected.

"That's the fun of it!" the Ruffles whined.

Little Wave was tempted, and he couldn't shake the Ruffles off. They were drawing him away.

Oh, what can it hurt? I'll come right back, he thought. So he let the Ruffles lead him away again.

Following the Ruffles, he heard a rumble
that quickly grew into a wild roar.

Soon he found himself in a dark place
where the wind screamed and giant
waves raged about, gnashing their teeth
and throwing spray from their crests.

The noise was terrific.
Little Wave was frightened.

"What do we do now?" he shouted above the din. But the Ruffles had disappeared.

Little Wave tried to back away, but it was no use. The howling winds pushed him. Mountainous billows tossed him back and forth. They growled menacingly at him, their angry green eyes glowing from their dark depths.

Suddenly a towering wave, bigger than all the rest, swept down on him. Trying to escape, Little Wave lost his balance and became completely embroiled in the storm. With a great crash, the monster buried him.

As he struggled against the seas around him, push-ing and thrashing furiously, he became part of the great noise himself.

It seemed to go on forever. Finally the storm abated. Tired and sore, Little Wave went wearily toward home.

He was disappointed in himself. How could he have left his faithful friend Old Swell again? Hadn't Little Wave been warned repeatedly not to listen to the Ruffles?

As before, when he reached Old Swell's side, the sage did not scold him. Instead, he spoke kindly.

"When we allow fear, anger, or desire to rule us, they can be very cruel masters."

Little Wave snuggled up to the side of his most beloved friend.

"Be still now," said Old Swell.

"I forget how, Master," Little Wave admitted.

"It's simple," Old Swell said. "Don't hurry; don't stop."

five

A New Name

Long after the storm had subsided,
Little Wave thought about Old
Swell's words.

Don't hurry; don't stop.

They seemed to be the clue to many
things—the mystery of being still,
the wonder of what a wave is,
the question of what is real
and what is not.

As he watched Old Swell rolling steadily across the sea, Little Wave thought about how the great Master embodied his own words.

No matter how many changes come and go, he thought, *Old Swell is always the same. He never hurries; he never stops.*

He sighed longingly. *If I could find the secret of* Don't hurry; don't stop, *maybe I wouldn't be tossed around so much.*

Little Wave moved closer to his teacher. "Master," he said, "teach me about *Don't hurry; don't stop.*"

Old Swell looked pleased. "There is a pace to your life," he said. "It is where the push from behind equals the pull from in front. Find that spot and stay within it."

Little Wave wanted to find his pace.

He didn't know how, but he was certain
it had something to do with Deep Listening.

Despite all his failures in the past,
he decided to try Deep Listening again.

It wasn't easy. At first, many thoughts came to his mind—about the Ruffles, the sparkles, and the storm. Each time it happened he told himself, *They are only what Old Swell calls a show.*

For a long time he heard nothing, but he kept on.

As he concentrated, he began to feel great peace. Then came a trickling of Joy. He was enjoying the trickle when he heard something like a faint hum.

He listened. The gentle hum grew louder. It seemed to rise out of the Great Deep. Soon it was all around him, but Little Wave was not frightened. He was glad.

Finally he was hearing the Sound.

Little Wave listened more carefully. He had never heard a sound like this before. And yet somehow he felt he had always heard it, there behind every other sound.

Ommm-m-m-m-m…

  Ommm-m-m-m-m…

As Little Wave listened, he realized the Sound was coming from inside him, all around him, everywhere. It was the *Voice of Everything.*

For a long, long time, Little Wave went on listening to the Sound.

It filled him with great comfort and helped him realize that he was more than he had ever thought he was.

Sometimes a strange feeling of being *larger* came over him.

"Master," he asked, "what is happening to me?"

Old Swell smiled. "You are becoming your true self. Not by escaping or competing are you doing so, but by obedience and through Deep Listening.

"You are changing. No longer are you Little Wave. Henceforth, you shall be known as *Small Swell*."

As Little Wave tried on his new
name, Small Swell, a quiet pride
spread through him.

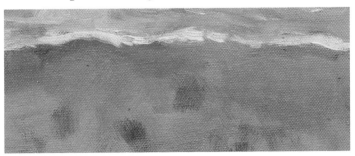

six

Destiny

Small Swell had been trying to concentrate on the Sound, but he was distracted by some curious noises coming from overhead.

Looking up, he saw many white birds circling and swooping.

He had seen birds before, but never so many. He watched them for a while. Behind their cries he heard a far-off surging. He turned toward the noise.

What he saw made his waters turn cold with fear. The dark line was now tall and menacing. Its form completely blocked the path of the waves.

"Master," he cried to Old Swell, "Destiny is almost upon us."

"Yes, my friend," Old Swell murmured
without a trace of fear or excitement.
In fact, Old Swell was smiling radiantly.
He seemed to glow with love.

Small Swell got as close to Old Swell as he could. Staring at the approaching dark mass, he noticed a broad flat band of pale yellow at its nearest edge.

He was looking, of course, at a sandy beach. As he watched, a large wave rose up and crashed onto the pale surface. Then it turned white, flattened out—and vanished!

"Look, Master," Small Swell cried. "See what is happening to waves that meet Destiny! When I meet Destiny, will it be the end of the Journey?"

Old Swell smiled. "Not an ending, my friend, but a returning."

Small Swell watched another of his fellow waves crash and dissolve on the edge of Destiny.

"What do you mean, Master?" he asked.

Old Swell answered with a question of his own. "Where did that last wave go?"

"It went back into the Great Deep," Small Swell said. Thinking about that, he felt better.

Suddenly he had another thought. *Does this mean that I will be a wave again?*

As always, Old Swell read his thoughts.
His voice was reassuring.

"You have been many waves. You will
be many waves. For what is a wave but
a part of the Great Deep that plays for
a little time in the show of things and
then returns to the place from whence
it came?"

Old Swell paused. Then he laughed and
said, "How else do you think I got to be
Old Swell?"

"Everything will be all right. Come, let us sing our song together." And Old Swell began to chant.

Soon all the waves around them were singing, too. As they neared Destiny, their song grew into a mighty chorus:

From Joy we came.
In Joy we live,
And in Thy sacred Joy
we will melt again.

Small Swell felt his beloved guide by his side, closer than ever. Somehow he knew that everything was all right, just as Old Swell had said.

As he joined his voice with the others, he finally understood.

Destiny loomed right in front of Little Swell, but he no longer had any fear.

What is there to fear? There is never a time when I am not a part of the Great Deep. I am only returning to where I came from.

Behind the surging of the waves, Small Swell heard the Voice of Everything. It seemed to come from everywhere.

And when at last he spilled onto the beach with a sigh—running up on the sands in tiny flowing eddies and sliding back again into the Great Deep—he felt only *Joy*.

And then came the biggest surprise of all. Although his waters were mingled with those of the Great Deep, he was still himself!

Looking around, he was happy to see many waves he had known before. Like himself, they had become underwater waves.

But what comforted him most of all was that Old Swell was there. He would always be there.

THE END

Help me to feel my connection

with the vast Ocean of Life,

the Oneness within all things.

Little Wave and Old Swell is inspired by the profound teachings of Paramahansa Yogananda, a great Indian sage who often compared the span of a human life to the rising and falling of an ocean wave.

Yogananda came to America in 1920. From that time until his passing in 1952, he lectured widely, wrote many books, and founded the Self-Realization Fellowship, an organization dedicated to disseminating his scientific techniques of yoga meditation.

Yogananda's inspirational books include *The Second Coming of Christ: The Resurrection of the Christ Within You* and the timeless, spiritual classic *Autobiography of a Yogi*.

Beyond Words Publishing, Inc.

OUR CORPORATE MISSION
Inspire to Integrity

OUR DECLARED VALUES

We give to all of life as life has given us.

We honor all relationships.

Trust and stewardship are integral to fulfilling dreams.

Collaboration is essential to create miracles.

Creativity and aesthetics nourish the soul.

Unlimited thinking is fundamental.

Living your passion is vital.

Joy and humor open our hearts to growth.

It is important to remind ourselves of love.